# DENVER
# DAYS

## BY SUE LUXA

D1277426

WESTERN REFLECTIONS
PUBLISHING COMPANY®

Montrose, Colorado

ISBN 1-890437-98-0
Library of Congress Control Number: 2003113339

First Edition
Printed in the United States of America

Cover illustration © 2004 by Joyce M. Turley,
    Dixon Cove Design
Cover and text design by Laurie Goralka Design

Western Reflections Publishing Company®
219 Main Street
Montrose, CO 81401
www.westernreflectionspub.com

*Dedicated to Melissa who had the idea.*

# TABLE OF CONTENTS

## Chapter 1
# THE JOURNEY BEGINS

Ten-year-old Katie O'Brien's nose was close against the train window as she watched the spinning landscape go by. She was looking forward to arriving in Denver before nightfall because someone special would be meeting her there . . . Aunt Clara Brown.

Katie thought she must have spent her entire life on trains. She thought about New York City, living as an orphan after her mother and father had died from pneumonia during the cold winter of 1881.

She had been placed on a passenger car that became part of the Orphan Train, which carried children without parents to parts of the Midwest to find homes in healthy climates and with new parents. They were often adopted by childless couples who treated the orphans as their own. There were also other children who were adopted because they provided free labor for the ranchers and farmers. They often lived much like servants without wages and very little to eat.

But Katie had been lucky to be adopted by a widow in Iowa. Mrs. Neal was a seamstress, trying to support herself after her husband, a Union soldier, had died in the Battle of Fredericksburg during the Civil War. She often spoke of her husband's belief that the South should not have left the United States. Even though she was still sad about his death, Mrs. Neal said, "He died for a good and just cause."

Katie wasn't so sure about the deaths of her parents. They had lived in a shabby, one-room walk-up apartment in New York City. Her parents had struggled to put food on the table for Katie and her younger brother, Joe.

Her father had worked in the streets, cleaning up the horse droppings and trying to keep the streets clean. It was backbreaking work, and Katie remembered how tired he would be when he returned home.

Katie's mother had taken in laundry and did sewing and ironing for the rich folks. With pain in her knees and legs, she would stand over the wash, rubbing the clothes until her hands were red and raw. Sometimes ten-year-old Katie would help her put the washed clothes through the ringer to get rid of the water. It was often that she and her mother would have clothes all over the two rooms of their apartment, waiting for them to dry so that Mother could iron them and have them ready for pickup in a few days.

Then the winter of 1881 had hit with its cold winds and temperatures. Her father came home with a hacking cough that often awakened Katie in the middle of the night. Before long, her mother was coughing, too. There wasn't money for a doctor. They couldn't stop working and, by February, Katie watched as her parents quickly became weaker and weaker.

A neighbor had felt sorry for her and Joe. She had taken Joe and Katie to the nearest orphanage where arrangements were made for both of them to join the Orphan Train, leaving the train depot for the Midwest.

Katie had been numb with grief, but she tried to stay strong for her little brother. "It won't be long till we find a grand place, Joe. We'll have food to eat and be able to play in the sunshine."

Joe wearily swung his too-small feet back and forth as he sat on the train seat with thirty other children on their way to new homes. Joe was a freckle-faced boy with reddish brown hair. As Katie watched him, she knew he would be quickly chosen because of his sweet smile and sad blue eyes. At six years of age, he had seen enough to make his eyes sad for the rest of his life. Katie was hoping he'd find a gentle home where there would be love. She also hoped that both of them would be adopted together. But that was not to be.

## Chapter 2
# A NEW LIFE IN THE WEST

When the train had stopped in Omaha, Nebraska, Joe had been scooped up and hugged by a young couple who were childless. Joe met all of their needs with his angelic face and red hair. Katie looked on, sadly hoping they would also choose her. Even though she was older, she told them she could help with chores and tend to her brother.

They shook their heads. "I'm really sorry, young lady. We're just starting out with housekeeping, and we can't afford another mouth to feed. We'd like to take you, but our wallets just won't allow it," stated the man matter-of-factly.

Just then a gray-haired woman of about sixty stepped forward to rest her chapped hand on Katie's shoulder.

"I couldn't help overhearing your need for a home and how handy you could be around the house. My name's Mrs. Neal. I'm in need of a good worker. I live in Council Bluffs, Iowa, just across the Missouri River from here. I heard there would be an Orphan Train stopping in Omaha. I have need of a good, strong worker. My legs and arms are starting to ache all the time. I do sewin' and laundry, so I could use two strong arms to help."

Katie watched as Joe walked off, hand in hand with the young couple. He glanced back at Katie and blinked back a tear, but Katie knew he would be happier without her.

She shrugged her shoulders and followed Mrs. Neal toward the waiting wagon. "I guess I could be some help to you. I know how the washin' goes 'cause my mother took in laundry in New York. I'm a quick learner, so the sewin' shouldn't be too hard. I've got strong hands and a willin' heart, so I guess I would be worth my food and the roof over my head." Mrs. Neal smiled wearily and put her hand on Katie's shoulder. "Perhaps livin' with Mrs. Neal wouldn't be so bad after all," thought Katie. She walked alongside Mrs. Neal as the gray-haired woman trudged toward the wagon that would take them to Council Bluffs.

They finally arrived in the Iowa town. Mrs. Neal drove to a small but neat little bungalow with a picket fence and a sagging gate. The two small windows at the front had gingham curtains tied back with pieces of twine. The house itself had once been white but now was in need of a good coat of whitewash. The neatly swept porch needed repair because the wood looked uneven. Katie could tell Mrs. Neal did the best she could with what she had. Maybe Mrs. Neal would do the best she could to provide for Katie, too.

"I'm not sure I should have pulled you from the other orphans." Katie looked up at Mrs. Neal with a questioning look. "What have I gotten myself into?" she thought. "I'm about ready to make a change in homes. I heard from a lady, a Mrs. Eliza Jane Brewer, who lives here in Council Bluffs. She has a sick mother, Aunt Clara Brown, in need of help. Only trouble is she lives in Denver, Colorado."

## Chapter 3
# ON THE WAY TO DENVER

So it was that Katie found herself on yet another train to yet another town. This time she was not with Joe, but Mrs. Neal. Katie thought about her little brother and knew he would be loved and cared for with his new family. She would have to find courage for her new adventure in Denver.

Katie had heard it was a bustling city with streets and carriages, with newspapers and businesses. Katie would just have to see what was there. Meanwhile she watched the dry, rolling plains go by, blurry and brown, from her train window.

Mrs. Neal was busy next to her with a bit of needle-work. She hardly ever had time to just sit and do what she enjoyed. Katie thought Mrs. Neal spent all of her time sewing and washing for others. Maybe when they got to Aunt Clara Brown's home, there would be more time for just relaxing.

Katie's stomach began to growl so loudly that Mrs. Neal looked over with a smile and reached for a satchel she had brought aboard. There was some food inside —

sandwiches, some dried apples, and a few pieces of cheese. Katie gobbled her sandwich quickly.

"I think you'd better find some water, young lady. You'll choke on your food," Mrs. Neal offered.

When Katie returned from asking the conductor for a paper cup of water, she noticed the gentleman sitting across the aisle from them. Katie thought he must be a rich man because he was dressed in a brown-checked suit with a matching vest underneath. Katie could just make out a gold watch chain that swung across his stomach and ended in a vest pocket. He must have a valuable watch hidden in that pocket.

Sure enough, just as Katie was looking at him, the man reached into his pocket and took out a gold watch. He flipped the watch's cover plate and looked impatiently at the time. Katie thought he must have an important meeting in Denver and was eager to arrive.

As Katie glanced at the man, she noticed a bowler hat on the seat beside him. Katie chuckled to herself. The man's hat really did look like a bowl turned upside down and glued to a brim with a brown silk ribbon around the bottom of the bowl. How strange!

Then Katie looked at the woman in the seat facing her and realized that women were just as silly with their clothing. The woman was in a dress of shiny black material with a high neck and dozens of white pearl buttons down the front.

"I wonder how long it took her to dress this morning," giggled Katie to herself.

But on top of the woman's head sat the silliest hat Katie had ever seen. It looked as if a bird had perched on the side of her hat. Every time the woman moved her head from side to side, the feathers would jump up and down and every which way. Some poor bird must have given its life in order to make that lady look so silly. "What a shame," thought Katie. Just as Katie was feeling sorry for the bird, Mrs. Neal pointed out the window.

"Just look at those mountains in the distance. They look so clear and white against the blue sky. No wonder people think this is the prettiest sight nature has given this land west of the Mississippi River," she exclaimed.

Katie, too, was thrilled with the foothills, stepping up to the rugged peaks of the Rocky Mountains. She knew she would love the mountains.

Mrs. Neal had assured her when they left Council Bluffs that people were the same everywhere one went. So maybe the people in New York City and Council Bluffs were the same as the people in Denver. There would be mean people, but there would also be those who would be kind. She hoped she would meet the kind ones.

## Chapter 4
# KATIE MEETS MRS. BROWN

The train whistle announced the flat plains of eastern Colorado had come to an end, and the sunny city of Denver was approaching. Katie left her thoughts and looked out once again to see many tracks leading into and out of Denver. People were crowding the platforms. The train came to a screeching stop as it pulled into Union Station. People were waiting for loved ones, for business friends. All eyes were glued to the train doors as the conductor stepped down with his stepstool to assist the passengers off the train.

Katie jumped down from the train step without any help from the conductor. It was Mrs. Neal who needed the conductor's hand as she limped down the steps. Katie guessed that she had rheumatism in her knees, and it made her joints achy and stiff.

In the distance, she saw a black woman. She was plump and wore a shiny, white-collared black dress and a crisp white turban on her head. She was smiling in Katie's and Mrs. Neal's direction.

Mrs. Neal caught the woman's smile and said, "That must be Mrs. Aunt Clara Brown, the lady we've come to care for."

Katie's mouth opened wide. Somehow she had not expected a dark-skinned lady needing help. In New York City, it had been the ex-slaves, freedmen and women who did all the heavy work that no one else wanted to do.

Katie's world was turning upside down. Her head was whirling from all the changes that were occurring.

*Aunt Clara Brown, the black woman who brought many freed slaves to Colorado.* Colorado Historical Society, F-3714

Somehow she hoped she would be staying here in Denver for a while. She wanted time to get used to this new place.

Aunt Clara Brown limped toward them with her cane. Katie followed shyly behind Mrs. Neal. As Clara Brown approached, she held out her hand to shake Mrs. Neal's hand. "Why, child, you can come out from behind this lady's skirts. I'm not goin' to bite."

Katie walked forward to curtsey. She wasn't quite sure what to do because Mrs. Neal had been singing the praises of Mrs. Brown ever since she had decided to come to Denver to care for this woman.

"Well, come on along. I'm mighty glad you've come all the way from Council Bluffs to watch over me. My daughter says you're a good worker, and that's all I need to know."

Clara Brown grabbed Katie's hand in her wrinkled one, and slipped her arm through Mrs. Neal's offered arm. They proceeded down the platform as others stared at the strange sight.

## Chapter 5

# A New Home in Denver

"I have a rented carriage outside for us to take," offered Mrs. Brown. "I thought I would have a special welcome for my two new friends from Council Bluffs."

Sure enough, there was a black, shiny carriage waiting with a driver on the front with whip and horse at the ready. He quickly hopped down to open the door for the three.

"Right this way, ladies," he gestured.

Katie felt special. She had never been treated with such respect. It must be nice to be rich enough to afford such transportation every day.

"Driver, please take us to Twenty-third and Arapahoe Street," stated Mrs. Brown firmly.

The driver gave a quick snap of the whip above the horse's head. They were off in a splendid carriage with black leather seats. Katie lovingly placed her hand on the leather and stroked it.

When they arrived at Mrs. Brown's home, Katie saw a small, square, white home with pink and white peony bushes in the front yard and a small porch with a rocking chair. Katie knew at once she would love this place. It was so neat and clean. Surely she and Mrs. Neal could keep up the place with sweeping, washing, and general house chores.

When they had entered the front door, Mrs. Brown said, "I'm sorry you'll have to share a room upstairs in the loft. I can't rightly climb those stairs without a lot of trouble, so you can find the place yourselves. There's fresh linen and the bed's a sturdy one, even though the coverlet's a bit raggedy."

Mrs. Neal and Katie carefully climbed a flight of steep, narrow stairs to the left of the doorway. Katie was glad there was a banister on the wall for holding. They twisted and turned until they reached the top. There was only one room that was sparsely furnished with a double bed and a patchwork quilt of many colors that was faded and old. There was a scratched dresser in the corner and a straight-backed wooden chair.

In another corner Katie noticed a much-used treadle sewing machine. There were spools of different colors on the edge of the sewing-machine ledge. The chair in front of the sewing machine was oddly shaped. There was a flat place for sitting but the arm rests curved up from the seat in one piece of wood. Katie thought it the most beautiful piece of furniture she had ever seen. She also knew her back would be mighty sore sitting at that machine for a long time because there was no backrest.

She would have to get used to the treadle sewing machine, because her short legs would have trouble reaching the piece underneath the machine that was moved up and down with one's foot. It took a steady action to keep that machine sewing straight seams.

Katie also noticed there was a flowered basin and bowl on the dresser with two white linen towels for Mrs. Neal and her to wash up in the mornings and evenings.

Mrs. Neal said, "I don't see any indoor plumbing. My guess is it must be outside in the backyard."

Sure enough, Katie glanced out the only window at a small wooden structure in the back. She pointed to the small wooden building.

"Yep, that's it," stated Mrs. Neal. "It'll be mighty cold going out there in the winter and mighty hot in the summer."

"Mrs. Neal, this is goin' to be perfect!" Katie said. "I've always had to share a bedroom with my whole family. Now, it'll be just you and me."

Mrs. Neal sighed. She wondered if she would be able to share a bed with a squirmy ten-year-old.

The year had been such a sad and changing one for Katie. Here it was 1882, and she had gone from New York to Omaha to Iowa to Denver, Colorado. As Mrs. Neal and Katie went down the stairs, there was Mrs. Brown with her cane in hand waiting to give them a tour of the tiny house.

*A Denver house similar to the one where Aunt Clara Brown lived.*
Denver Public Library, Western History Department, X-25747

## Chapter 6
# BARNEY FORD VISITS AUNT CLARA

Just then there was a quiet knock at the front door. Mrs. Brown hobbled to the door and turned the knob. Curiously, Katie looked around the old lady's billowing skirt and saw a light-skinned gentleman, hat in hand, smiling at Aunt Clara.

"Why, Mr. Ford, come in. Come in."

Katie noticed Mr. Ford wore a brown wool suit with a white handkerchief peeking out from his left-front chest pocket. He had a white bushy mustache and a goatee hugging his chin.

"Well, Barney Ford, aren't you a sight for sore eyes! Come on in and meet my new helpers. After all these years of helpin' others, I'm now needin' some care myself. These old legs just don't get around as fast as they used to."

The man entered and followed Clara to the parlor. "Come on in, Katie. You, too, Mrs. Neal. I want you to meet a dear friend of mine. This here's Barney Ford, owner of the People's Restaurant down at Fifteenth and

Blake. He and I are rare ones — we're both colored folk, we're both pioneers, and we've both been slaves."

Mrs. Neal blushed red to hear Clara talk so openly about her slave days. She thought Aunt Clara would be embarrassed about such a past. Instead Clara Brown seemed proud that she had overcome slavery and was now a freedwoman.

"How's business, Barney?" It was Ford who owned and operated, not only a restaurant, but also a barbershop in a two-story brick building. He was the son of a slave and had escaped slavery on the Underground Railway, a series of safe homes where slaves could hide. They would travel from home to home in the dark and sleep during the day. He was one of the lucky ones to escape, but knew his fortune was to be made in the West.

He came to Denver in 1860, shortly after the discovery of gold. Even though his first business had gone up in flames in 1863, he had built an even better business. He also built the Inter-Ocean Hotel at Sixteenth and Blake Streets.

Katie could tell that Aunt Clara admired Ford's business sense, because she, too, had had to struggle in Central City, washing and cleaning the miners' dirty clothes. Slowly, but surely, she had built up a small fortune, just like Barney Ford.

"It's goin' fine, Mrs. Brown. The barbershop is as busy as ever, too. That's where I heard you're feelin' poorly."

"These old legs don't seem to have the get-up-and-go they used to have. I guess all of those years on my knees doin' laundry and scrubbin' have just caught up with me," stated Clara.

"I wanted you to know there are lots of us in the Pioneer Association who are willin' to help out any way we can. Just give a whistle and we'll be here."

"I thank you kindly, Barney. I'll certainly do that. But I've hired on two ladies from Council Bluffs where my daughter Eliza Jane lives. She's sent me Mrs. Neal and her new girl, Katie O'Brien, to help with my needs."

Mrs. Neal and Katie both smiled shyly at the dapper gentleman, sitting in the brown horsehair sofa near the fireplace. Soon Katie began to fidget. The horsehair in the sofa was scratchy to the touch and it definitely was uncomfortable to sit on. Katie thought that people didn't want their guests to stay long if they had such bumpy furniture.

"I got to be goin', Mrs. Brown. I just wanted to stop in and wish you well," stated Barney Ford.

"I know you're mighty busy, so I'm glad you took time away from business to drop by. You take care of yourself, you hear?" said Aunt Clara kindly.

## Chapter 7
# AUNT CLARA TELLS HER STORY

A s the days and weeks went by, Katie found Aunt Clara to be a caring lady with many friends who dropped in to talk and find out how ill she was. As always, Aunt Clara was in good spirits and cheered up the people who came to visit.

Katie still thought about the day that Barney Ford had visited and wanted to ask him about his days of slavery. All the stories she had read about the Civil War and slavery had been sad tales of black people who had worked for plantation owners who were often cruel. Of course, there was never any pay, and the slaves lived in small wooden shacks with barely any furniture and bedding.

One day as Aunt Clara was rocking in her chair by the parlor window, Katie slipped in and sat down in the nearby chair.

"Aunt Clara, I've been wonderin' about that day Mr. Ford came to see you."

"Yes, honey, what is it you've been wonderin'?" asked Aunt Clara.

"You mentioned that both of you had been slaves. I was hopin' you might be willin' to tell me somethin' about your life as a slave?"

"I can say it wasn't the happiest time of my life because I was sold away from my husband and four children. I reckon I was born in the early 1800s in Virginia or Tennessee. There aren't many good records of slaves' births, but as near as I can tell, that was my birthday. I do remember the War of 1812, so I'm a mighty old lady now. I'm guessin' in my eighties somewhere.

"I moved to Kentucky when I was about nine, and I was married at eighteen. I was proud to have four children, three girls and one boy. When my owner died, my children and I were sold. I never did see my husband again. My children were sold, too. Those were sad days for Aunt Clara.

"My last master, Mr. Brown, freed me before he died. In 1859 I came West with a wagon train to make my fortune. I went up to Central City, along with some of the early prospectors, but I didn't get money from the gold and silver mines. No, siree, I earned my money with my hands. I took in laundry, saved my money, and bought land and houses in Central City. But I'm proudest of havin' been one of the founders of the St. James Church up there. It gave lots of hope to the families tryin' to make a livin' from those mines. My house burned down. I regret not bein' very good at readin' and writin'. I had to work so hard I never had the time to learn. Now that I can't move around very easily, I wish I could read the papers and magazines.

"The scariest day I had was when I was climbin' a hill in Central City, deliverin' some laundry to a customer when I could hardly breathe. Old Aunt Clara had to sit down on the side of the road. Some kind folks saw me huffin' and puffin' and took me back to my cabin. The doctor said it was my heart, and I needed to move to a lower altitude. I was goin' on eighty years of life, so I decided to move down to Denver. I know Denver's a mile high, but at least it's better than Central City. So here I am — right here with you and Mrs. Neal, feelin' a lot better."

Aunt Clara sighed and then said, "All in all I guess I've had a good life — interestin', anyway, but I've also had my share of heartaches, too."

"I'm sorry to hear about all your troubles, and I wish your heart was better. You've had a lot of things happen to you, Aunt Clara. You must certainly be a rich lady with all the money you made from the laundry business and all the property you owned," blurted out Katie.

Aunt Clara laughed until her sides were achy and tears ran down her cheeks.

"I wouldn't say that, missy. I spent part of my money lookin' for my family. I traveled back to Kentucky where my last master had lived. I searched, only to learn that two of my children had died. I never could find my boy, but I brought sixteen freed men and women to Colorado to start a new life.

"But the best thing happened just a year or so ago. A friend of mine, Becky Johnson, was visitin' in Council Bluffs, Iowa. She went to a church supper and met a Missus Brewer there. After talkin' to her for awhile, Mrs. Johnson put two and two together. She knew this must be my own Eliza Jane. I was never so thrilled as when I learned about Eliza Jane. I could hardly wait to see her. But that's a story for another time, young lady."

Katie's mouth must have been wide open with this new story Aunt Clara told.

"Why, child, you look as if the cat's got your tongue," laughed the old lady.

Katie remembered to close her mouth. "I think you must be a very special lady. I know now why so many people visit you and love you. I can't believe you were able to do all that."

"Why it's not hard when you set your mind to it," she chuckled. "Now you get on back to work with Mrs. Neal while I warm my old bones here in the sun." Her eyes glazed over with a faraway look, and Katie knew she was dreaming about other days and memories.

## Chapter 8
# A Delicious Treat

One day Aunt Clara limped into the kitchen where Mrs. Neal and Katie were fixing lunch. She had a gleam in her eye, and Katie knew something exciting was going to happen.

"Ladies, I think I should tell you there's an ice-cream shop down on Larimer Street. It's named Baur's. They have delicious sodas and pastries," Aunt Clara invited.

"What's a soda?" asked Katie.

"Why, child, it's the sweetest drink this side of the Mississippi River. It's made with thick cream and fizzy water. The bubbles tickle your nose, and the taste makes your stomach feel good for hours."

Katie's eyes lit up. She could remember the candies her parents would give her and her brother when there were a few extra pennies. Now she was trying to imagine how tasty a soda would be.

"Child, I want you to go down to Larimer and get us three sodas — one for you, one for Mrs. Neal, and one for me. My sweet tooth is callin' for one of those creamy sodas."

Katie ran to the hallway, grabbed her brown wool coat off the coat rack, and waited for Aunt Clara to give her the change for the treats. "Take this pitcher for the drinks, step lively, and don't spill a drop," cautioned Aunt Clara.

Katie sped to the Larimer address, based on directions from Aunt Clara, and sure enough, there was the sign that said Baur's. She stopped to get her breath, opened the door, and was greeted by all kinds of sweets. "This must be the best place in Denver," she thought.

On the shelves were all kinds of glasses for ice cream and sodas. In the glass cases were different kinds of candies. It was a dream come true.

"What'll you have, miss?" asked the man behind the counter.

"I'll have three sodas. Please put them in this pitcher," stated Katie.

The soda man looked a bit unsure. "We don't usually do that. Most of the people just eat right here in the store."

"But I'm gettin' this for Mrs. Clara Brown on Arapahoe Street."

"Oh, that's different. She's a mighty fine lady and has helped so many people." "Did everyone know Aunt Clara?" thought Katie.

"Here you go, miss."

Katie paid the clerk and walked slowly to the door, trying not to spill a drop. She could hardly wait to get home. Katie imagined she could already taste the sweet potion.

When she arrived home, Mrs. Neal was waiting to open the door. Katie suspected she was as excited as Katie was about the treat.

"Let's sit down and enjoy the sodas," said Aunt Clara, peering around Mrs. Neal.

They got spoons and napkins and three glasses. Mrs. Neal gently poured the liquid into the three glasses and gave each a spoon.

For a good ten minutes the only sound in Aunt Clara's kitchen was the sound of slurping and "ahs" from all three. Now that Katie knew about Baur's she was not soon to forget how to get there. She was already hoping Aunt Clara would make this a regular event. Her sweet tooth was still twitching!

## Chapter 9

# TUMBLEWEEDS

The winds of December, 1882, began to blow, and Katie's mind turned to thoughts of Christmas. Aunt Clara had said nothing about decorating. Katie knew she was a church woman, so the season would be important to her.

One day Katie again found Aunt Clara in front of the window, watching the people and carriages go by.

"Have you thought much about Christmas, Aunt Clara?"

"Oh, child, I been givin' it lots of thought. It's time for us to begin makin' this house look ready for the season. I usually have a tree with candles and ornaments, but I don't think I'm up to it this year. My old joints are always stiff when the weather gets cold."

"I could do it, Aunt Clara," Katie burst out.

"Do you really think you're up to all that work, girl?"

"I bet Mrs. Neal would help me."

"You go ahead and see what you can come up with, missy," Aunt Clara said as she gazed out the window.

The tumbleweeds had been blowing into town from the prairie. Katie had heard people complaining about finding the bushy dried weeds in their yards. The same had been true for Aunt Clara's home. Katie had picked them up one by one to be burned in the fireplace on cold winter days.

As she stepped outside the house one blustery day, Katie saw a bunch of the weeds go whooshing by. Somehow she thought about having to pick up yet more tumbleweeds. Then a thought struck her: "Why not use these good-for-nothin' weeds for Christmas decoration?" She ran toward the street and grabbed up two of the biggest bushes, dusted them off and walked into the house carrying one in each hand.

"What do you have there, Katie?" asked Mrs. Neal, wiping her hands on her apron as she came from the kitchen.

"I have two tumbleweeds for Christmas," announced Katie proudly

"And what do you hope to do with those ugly old things?"

"I'm goin' to make Christmas!"

"And how do you propose to do that?"

"I'm goin' to decorate these tumbleweeds and put one on top of the other so that we have an honest-to-goodness Christmas tree."

"I never heard of such an idea, but it just might work. We can't use any candles because the dry weeds would go up in fire, but we could string rows of popcorn. Maybe we could even make some decorations."

"Aunt Clara says she has decorations. I wonder if she'll like this?" said Katie.

"I sure do think it's a grand idea," stated Aunt Clara from the parlor entrance. "It's just different enough to be lots of fun."

Katie beamed to think she'd thought of this idea all by herself. It would be so much fun to have a tree that was different from everyone else's tree.

Katie, Mrs. Neal, and Aunt Clara set to work popping popcorn and stringing it on thread from Aunt Clara's sewing basket. With colored paper they cut out white stars, red stockings and green wreaths to hang on the tumbleweeds. Aunt Clara had placed a white doily on her oak claw-footed table in the parlor. Then Katie climbed up on a chair and carefully placed one tumbleweed on top of the other. She decorated the tree with the popcorn strings and the colored ornaments. Aunt Clara and Mrs. Neal looked on from below and gave her encouragement and advice about where to hang the ornaments.

"It's a mighty fine tree, if I do say so myself," huffed Aunt Clara.

Katie's eyes twinkled to think she had come up with this idea all by herself. Christmas might be special this year after all.

## Chapter 10
# A CHRISTMAS TO REMEMBER

It was a *special* Christmas. Aunt Clara smiled every time she looked at the homemade tree that the three of them had put together. Friends dropped over for warm punch and chewy cookies. Aunt Clara almost seemed to forget her aches during the holiday.

"It's at times like this that I give thanks for what I have. Time may be catchin' up with me, but there is still lots that I can do — with the help of my two ladies, of course." Katie felt proud that Aunt Clara thought so highly of Mrs. Neal and her.

Mrs. Neal had bought a gift just for Katie, and she handed it to her. "I hope you like it, Katie. You've been such a help to me and Mrs. Brown, with nary a complaint comin' from your lips."

Katie took the gift with a smile, but eagerly tore at the wrapping. Inside the paper was a bank, not just any bank, but a cast-iron mechanical bank with a bird perched atop a church, complete with beautiful stained glass windows.

"Here's your first coin to put inside," Mrs. Neal said as she took a nickel from her apron pocket and handed it to Katie. She placed it in the bird's topknot and released a lever and watched as the bird moved forward, leaned over the church chimney, and dropped the coin into the church.

Katie squealed with delight. "Now I know what to do with the money Aunt Clara has been payin' me. It won't be long before I'll have enough money for somethin' really special. I haven't decided exactly what, but I'll know it when I see it."

"Aunt Clara, Mrs. Neal and I have something for you. It's a Christmas present," Katie offered.

"Why, that was surely a sweet thing to do," Aunt Clara said as she reached for the gift. As she tore the wrapping paper, she said, "I do declare, this is the prettiest blanket anyone's ever made for me. It's goin' to keep me warm in front of the window on cold winter days."

Katie and Mrs. Neal had sewed together scraps of fabric to make a patchwork lap robe for Aunt Clara. It had been practice for Katie to sew the patches together with the sewing machine upstairs. She knew there were mistakes, but Aunt Clara didn't seem to mind a bit.

"I haven't forgotten you two, either," beamed the white-haired lady.

She gave Katie and Mrs. Neal identical packages. Katie was faster at opening her gift. "Why, it's chocolates from Baur's!" exclaimed Katie. She could feel her mouth watering for one of those candies. "But how could you have gotten them? It bein' so difficult for you to walk?"

"Now don't you worry, child. Aunt Clara has her ways."

Katie looked over at Mrs. Neal. Her mouth was full of the sweet candy, and her lips were smudged with chocolate. But there was a smile on her face that was as big as could be.

## Chapter 11

# AUNT CLARA TELLS ABOUT OLD DENVER

"Tell me a story about old Denver, Aunt Clara," asked Katie one cold February day in 1883 when snow covered the ground, and she couldn't get outside to run errands.

"Well, let's see. There are so many stories about Denver. It has been such a wild and wooly town for the miners, the immigrants, and the riffraff that have passed through Denver. Old Union Depot down on Wynkoop Street has helped to bring a crowd of people who think they're goin' to strike it rich here. They built that station just a couple years ago, around 1881 I suspects and already Denver is bustin' at the seams with new folks.

"There are always scalawags waitin' for the unsuspectin' folk who come here for the gold in the mountains. They know the gold that was found here around 1858 is played out. It was that old William Russell and his band of fellas from Auraria, Georgia, that first found gold near the South Platte River and Cherry Creek.

"Then, of course, there was William McGaa and John Simpson Smith, who arrived in Denver City about the same time and are considered its founders. But for my money it was General William Larimer who founded Denver City when he staked his claim and formed the Denver City Town Company. I'm afraid too many men lost their land at the gamblin' tables or as grubstakes in the gold fields. It was that old lure, 'Pikes Peak or Bust.' It wasn't long before Auraria and Denver joined together so's they could fight off Golden's claim to bein' the biggest town in the area.

"Denver was named for James Denver, the governor of the Kansas Territory. Then Denver started to grow so fast with prospectors and businessmen that the federal government named it the Colorado Territory in 1861. People around here say there was close to one thousand people here in 1860.

"This was the nearest city, besides San Francisco, out in the West, so it was important for that Union Depot to get built. We can't just depend on gold to keep this town goin'. We've got to raise food, have bakeries and grocery stores, meat packin' and farm equipment. This town is goin' to be the biggest and best place to live in just a few years. You just mark my words.

"Anyway, back to my story: The men comin' in on the trains at Union Depot often lost their money. There'd be scoundrels waitin' for them at the depot, promisin' all kinds of wealth. With promises of riches, they'd take the unsuspectin' men to a nearby hotel. The newcomers would sign papers or who knows what else, and before they knew it, they were poor, and the scoundrels had taken off with their money. Many a business has gotten its workers from the gold seekers who were flummoxed. It's a mighty sad tale, but you always have to look out for someone who wants to separate you from your money."

Katie laughed to hear such a story, but then she thought of the coins she was saving in her bank and decided maybe it wasn't so funny after all.

"Isn't there anyone in Denver who loves this town just because it's so close to the snowy mountains and the shiny blue sky?" asked Katie.

"I reckon the closest man to all of that would be William Byers. He's a big man in town, although he's retired from work now. He's gettin' along in years, just like old Aunt Clara.

"William Byers came to Denver near the beginnin', about 1859 I suspects. He opened a newspaper office, *The Rocky Mountain News*, on the second floor of Dick Wooten's grocery store on April 23, 1859. He printed his newspaper on anythin' he could find — brown wrappin' paper, pink tissue paper, even wallpaper — because it was sometimes hard to get paper from back East. He sold that paper for twenty- five cents a copy or five dollars for a year.

"Later he moved his newspaper to the middle of Cherry Creek and built it on stilts. It didn't help much because it was washed away and Mr. Byers along with it, in the 1860s. This didn't bother old William. He just up and built another office.

"Between floods and fires this town is always livin' on the edge. Now the city's talkin' about buildin' a fire-hose company over on Chestnut and Twentieth Street. There're so many wood shacks around that we're just askin' for another fire whenever someone gets careless with a candle or kerosene.

"Anyway back to my story: Old Byers was the best spokesman for Denver and Colorado. He wrote guide-books for people in the East. Of course, all of his stories weren't always true. One of the stories he liked to tell was about Denver's bein' the steamboat capital of the West. Can you imagine that? Here we are with just Cherry Creek and the South Platte, and the water certainly isn't deep enough to float a big steamboat. Even so, he sure fooled a lot of people with that one. Now he's buildin' a big house for his family way up on Thirteenth and Bannock.

"To Byer's credit, he did offer free seeds to anyone who stopped in at his office and was a great believer in farmin' on this dry land. Oh, and his wife, Mrs. Byers, is a mighty fine lady. She helps out with the needy folks. She and Mrs. John Evans started the Ladies' Relief Society, the Old Ladies' Home, the Denver Children's Home, the Young Women's Christian Association, and the United Way. I'd say Mrs. Byers is a busy lady and mighty kind to others who are down on their luck.

"Yes, I'd say Mr. and Mrs. Byers are probably the best known couple in these parts, except for, maybe, Horace and Baby Doe Tabor. But that's a story for another time. Old Aunt Clara wants to take a nap right now. So you get on about your chores while I snooze here in the sun."

Katie wrapped the patchwork blanket more tightly around Aunt Clara and tiptoed out of the parlor.

## Chapter 12

# A TRIP TO THE BUTCHER SHOP AND MR. BYERS, HIMSELF

"Katie, oh, Katie, come here would you?" called Aunt Clara from the parlor.

Katie rushed in from the kitchen, braked to a stop in front of Aunt Clara, and caught her breath.

"Child, you didn't have to come *that* fast. I'd like for you to run another errand for old Aunt Clara. I have it in mind to have a good fresh cut of roast beef. Every once in awhile my taste buds get the better of me. Just like that soda from Baur's, now I want some beef.

"Old George Kettle has a butcher shop down on Larimer. I know it's a far piece for you to walk, but you've got young legs. It's just a small shop at 1426, but it's got a fancy stone front. I bet if you tell Mr. Kettle the meat's for Aunt Clara, he'll give you a special roast."

Katie skipped down the street on her way to Larimer. She remembered the story Aunt Clara had told about General Larimer, so she guessed the street had been named in his honor.

She was having so much fun thinking of old Denver that she almost missed George Kettle's butcher shop. It looked to be only about twenty feet wide with a special carved beam across the top of the door. Katie guessed Mr. Kettle wanted to announce to all his customers just where to find his store since it was so tiny.

Katie opened the door and saw in front of her a sparkling white glass-fronted counter. Inside was the most meat Katie had ever seen at one time. There were chickens. There was pork. There was lamb. Over on one side Katie even saw slabs of cheese.

Suddenly her mouth began to water. She could just taste that delicious meat when Mrs. Neal cooked it. It had been a long time since she had had a real roast beef. Because her family had been so poor, they had lived on sausages and potatoes and beans.

This would even be better than Christmas when Mrs. Neal had fixed a chicken for their meal. Bless Aunt Clara, she really knew how to make a child's taste buds perk up.

There were several customers waiting their turn in line. But before too long it was Katie's turn.

"What can I do for you, young lady?" the butcher behind the counter inquired.

"I'm here on an errand for Mrs. Clara Brown," Katie said importantly.

"How's that fine lady doing these days? I hear she's been rather sickly."

Katie beamed and said, "Mrs. Neal and I are carin' for her, and she's doin' just fine right now, as long as she remembers to take her medicine. She still has trouble walkin', but she's as kind as ever."

"Good to hear, good to hear. But what does she want from old George Kettle?"

"Oh, you're George Kettle. Mrs. Brown told me to ask for you specially. She wants a good cut of roast beef for our dinner tonight. I can hardly wait!"

"I think we can manage that," Mr. Kettle said as he grabbed for a piece of paper and slid open the cabinet. "This looks like a fine piece of meat. I'll wrap it up with butcher paper and string. Just a minute."

"Miss," there was a voice coming from the corner of the store near the cheeses. "I couldn't help but overhear you talking about Mrs. Clara Brown. I'm one of her biggest fans. You probably don't know me, but I'm William Byers. I used to work at *The Rocky Mountain News.*"

"I know who you are," stated Katie. "You didn't just work at *The News,* you were *The News.* Mrs. Brown has told me what a cheerleader you've been for Denver, how people from the East came here to Denver just on your say so and how you started your newspaper on next-to-nothing."

The gray-haired gentleman with a beard blushed and seemed pleased to hear that Aunt Clara thought highly of him. "I'm not sure about that, but I do know I love Denver. I think it really is 'The Queen City of the Plains.' I know there are great things in store for it. We've got four railroads coming into Denver right now. There are newcomers arriving every day, and they're not just coming for the gold, either. They want to build a life out here. If the East ever finds out about our mild, dry climate and wide open spaces, there's no telling how many more will come. Oh, I know we get a bit of snow and sometimes it's more like a blizzard, but I think folks will know the rest of the year is just great. Wait till they see our fall — the prettiest you've ever seen with those gold aspens in the mountains. Why our fall could go on until November if we're lucky."

Katie kept nodding her head, waiting for Mr. Byers to take a breath. It was clear he was a good spokesman for Denver. "I'm sorry, Mr. Byers, but I have to get this beef home to Mrs. Neal before it spoils," Katie interrupted. She paid Mr. Kettle the money for the meat and walked toward the door.

"Say, why don't I walk with you to see Mrs. Brown? Now that I'm retired I have more time on my hands. About the only thing I do nowadays is my Denver postmaster job. When time hangs heavy on my hands I watch my house being built up on Bannock Street. It's going to be a humdinger, if I do say so myself. Some day I want to write a history of this great state. I'm thinking of calling it *The Encyclopedia of Biography of Colorado*. It's going to be a long one — several volumes, I suspect. My writing plans will have to wait awhile until I finish my job at the post office."

"There he goes again," thought Katie. "There's no stoppin' this man."

As Katie walked and Mr. Byers talked, they quickly arrived on Arapahoe Street and headed up to Aunt Clara's front porch.

Katie knocked on the door because she was having trouble with the meat. Mrs. Neal appeared at the door, wiping her hands on her apron. She looked surprised to see the stranger standing in front of her.

"This is Mr. Byers, Mrs. Neal. He's come to say 'hello' to Aunt Clara."

"Why, that lady has so many friends it's hard to keep track of all of them. Come in, Mr. Byers. I'll take your hat, and you go on into the parlor. Mrs. Brown's sittin' by the window. I bet she's already seen you come up the path," Mrs. Neal said.

Sure enough, there was Aunt Clara, rocking in her chair and smiling from ear to ear. "Mr. Byers, what a sight for sore eyes. Katie and I were just talkin' about you the other day, and I was sayin' what a fine gentleman you are."

"You, Mrs. Brown, know how to turn a man's head. I wanted to see how you're doing. The word around town is that you're feeling poorly."

"I have two new helpers in my house now, Mr. Byers. You've met Mrs. Neal and Katie. They've been the best thing to happen to me in many a day. I don't think I could get along without them.

"The doctor says I have to take it easy. He says I've got dropsy. My ankles swell somethin' awful sometimes. That's why it's hard for me to walk much anymore."

"I know Julia Greeley is looking in on you, and that's a good thing. Even though she has only one eye, she was a right good nurse for Governor Gilpin's family when he was the first governor of the Colorado Territory.

"I just wish everyone could know about your good works — all the churches and Sunday schools you started here in Denver, and all the people who have received money from you. It makes me wonder how you ever had time to do all your good deeds. One of these days the people will give you a proper thank-you for all your work."

"Mr. Byers, I only did what I thought I should. I've been so blessed to find my family after all these years. I came from slavery in a wagon train to these parts when everythin' was unsettled. I worked and worked to make a livin' in the gold towns, and I wanted to share it with those who haven't been so lucky."

"Mrs. Brown, I'm proud to know you, and I know the people of Denver are lucky to have you. I'd best be going, so I don't tire you. It's been good to see you."

"I thank you kindly for your visit. We're two of the old settlers. We've seen a lot of changes in Denver, that's for sure."

Mr. Byers backed out of the parlor, grabbed his hat from the coat rack in the corner and let himself out of the door.

## Chapter 13
# A VISIT FROM HORACE AND BABY DOE TABOR

A s spring came and went, the days began to turn warm. It wasn't long until June popped up on the calendar. That was the month Katie would long remember. Mrs. Neal and she had gotten into a routine of cooking, washing, and cleaning. If Katie worked it right, she would usually have a couple hours in the afternoon to herself. Often she found it was fun to spend time with Aunt Clara.

One day when Katie was finishing her chores, there was a knock on the door. It was Horace and Baby Doe Tabor. Katie remembered seeing pictures of the couple in the newspapers. Mr. Tabor's grand opera house was the talk of the neighborhood. She couldn't believe such rich people would be visiting Aunt Clara's little house.

Katie's mouth was open, as well as the door, when she glanced at this finely dressed couple. Baby Doe with her curls and baby-doll mouth was dressed in silk with one of those silly bustles in the back of her dress. Katie always thought if a woman fell backwards in a bustle, she

*Horace Tabor, the man who gave the money for the Tabor Grand Opera House.*
Denver Public Library, Western History Department, X-22028

*Baby Doe Tabor, the second wife of Horace Tabor, the mining businessman.*
Colorado Historical Society, F-737

would bounce right back up. Such a dress decoration was funny. She tried not to laugh.

Horace was decked out in a black suit with a small bow tie, but it was his huge handlebar mustache that caught Katie's eye: bushy, brown, and waxed at the ends into curls. Such foolishness! Why did rich people dress in such strange fashions?

"Please come in. I know you are the Tabors."

"Yes, we are, and we wish to see Mrs. Brown," stated Mr. Tabor, who seemed used to giving directions.

Katie led them into the parlor and announced, "It's Mr. and Mrs. Horace Tabor to see you, Aunt Clara."

"Why, I do declare. I never expected to see you at old Aunt Clara's simple house. Come in. Come in and sit a spell."

The Tabors sat on the edge of the horsehair sofa. Katie noticed they, too, didn't seem to be comfortable sitting on that old bumpy sofa.

"Mrs. Brown, we've come to offer you tickets to the Tabor Grand Opera House for a performance by the Theodore Thomas Orchestra on June 19. He is supposed to have one of the largest musical groups in the country. We certainly wanted him to play for us in Denver in my Tabor Grand Opera House," Mr. Tabor said proudly.

"But I can't afford a seat at such a fine event," Aunt Clara protested.

"You miss my meaning, Mrs. Brown. I want to give you tickets for the performance. Perhaps you could even bring your little helper here," he said, pointing to Katie.

Strangely enough, Mrs. Neal appeared in the parlor on tiptoes to hear the conversation. Katie thought she must have been listening and didn't want to lose a chance to see the Tabor Grand Opera House. The opera house had been the talk of Denver since it opened in 1881. People raved about the huge theater and how expensive it was to see the performances.

"Why I see you have another worker in your house. By all means, bring that lady standing in the doorway. I'll leave three tickets for you. How's that?"

"It's more generous than I could ever hope for," spluttered Aunt Clara. "I thank you kindly for your charity."

"After all you've done for the folks in Central City and Denver, I thought you deserved a special afternoon out on the town." Mr. Tabor had a twinkle in his eyes. Katie knew he must be as generous as Aunt Clara.

The Tabors rose to leave and bowed slightly to Aunt Clara in her rocking chair.

"We'll see you on the nineteenth, Mrs. Brown," Mrs. Tabor said as they left.

Katie squealed. She jumped up and down until Aunt Clara said, "Hush, child, you're goin' to give me a headache with all that bouncin' around."

"We're goin' to the theater! We're goin' to the theater! I can hardly wait!" exclaimed Katie. Already, her mind was thinking of what she would wear. She didn't really have a fine dress, but she knew Mrs. Neal would sew one for her.

"Oh, Mrs. Neal, I feel just like Cinderella. I hope you'll be my fairy godmother. Would you make a special dress for me to wear?"

"I just might do that, young lady, if I can get some work out of you in the kitchen. It's almost time for dinner."

## Chapter 14

# A SPECIAL AFTERNOON AT THE TABOR GRAND OPERA HOUSE

K atie looked at herself in the standing mirror in the corner of the entryway. She twirled and twisted to get the best view of her new dress. Mrs. Neal had kept her promise and made her a shiny green skirt with a tight-fitting shirtwaist in the same fabric. Mrs. Neal had even put a ruffle at the bottom of the skirt. Katie wore her black socks and black, lace-up shoes.

Mrs. Neal had brushed Katie's long red hair until it gleamed. Then she pulled back her hair with a green ribbon. Katie was thrilled. It was going to be an exciting afternoon at the Tabor Grand Opera House.

Aunt Clara and Mrs. Neal came to the door, ready to leave. It was so hot that there was no need for wraps. Katie began to feel warm in her dress. She noticed that Aunt Clara and Mrs. Neal also looked damp and warm in the hot summer air.

Even so, Katie skipped along beside the women. Aunt Clara had refused to take a carriage, so Mrs. Neal was holding her arm as both ladies limped down the street toward Sixteenth and Curtis where the Tabor Grand Opera House stood.

Katie could see it in the distance with its tall turret and five stories. It was the grandest building she had ever seen. Even the New York City buildings that she remembered weren't as eye-catching as this one: to Katie, it looked like a castle.

When the trio entered the theater, Katie couldn't believe what she was seeing. She could hardly believe the splendor — the gold, the sparkling chandelier, the mural on the stage, and the rounded box seats three tiers high where the rich and famous people could sit. Now she really *did* feel like Cinderella.

Because Aunt Clara was a woman of color, she and her guests were not allowed to sit in the lower level. They were forced to walk up flights of stairs to the upper level for their seats. It was difficult for Aunt Clara to walk. Katie thought Mr. Tabor should have allowed Aunt Clara to sit in the lower area. This wasn't the kind Mr. Tabor she remembered.

Suddenly all was hushed. Katie looked over the railing and saw the Tabors enter the box seats in the first tier that had been banked with white lilacs. Mrs. Tabor's arm was firmly entwined in her husband's arm. Mrs. Tabor sat down in a small chair. It almost looked like a child's chair.

Katie guessed the special chair had been made for Baby Doe because she was so short, only about five feet tall. Mr. Tabor looked at friends and nodded. He sat down just as the orchestra began to play. Katie thought it was almost as if a king and queen had entered the theater.

When the orchestra played, Katie forgot about the Tabor's welcome and his rudeness toward Aunt Clara. When Belle Cole began to sing, Katie closed her eyes and really did believe she was in paradise.

*The Tabor Opera House where Katie, Aunt Clara Brown, and Mrs. Neal went to see a performance.*
Colorado Historical Society, CHS-J2549

## Chapter 15

# AUNT CLARA SETS
# KATIE STRAIGHT

For many days the only thing Katie could talk about was the music and songs at the Tabor Grand Opera House. Aunt Clara would just rock and rock at the parlor window, nod her head, and say, "Yes, ma'am, it surely was grand."

But one day Katie, sitting at Aunt Clara's swollen feet, asked her about the Tabors. "Tell me the story of Baby Doe and Horace Tabor. I noticed that some people looked away from them when they entered the theater the other day. It was as if they were ashamed of them."

"It is a miracle story, but it has its sadness, too. I feel sorry for Mr. Tabor's first wife, Augusta. He divorced her to marry Baby Doe. Some people do not approve of his new wife. Everyone loves them for what they have done for Denver and Leadville, but they don't like that he wasn't kind to his first wife."

"I thought it was mean of him to give you tickets that were so far away up the stairs in the opera house. He knows you have a difficult time walkin'. He could have let us sit downstairs," remarked Katie in a hurt voice.

Aunt Clara cupped Katie's chin in her hand. "Look at me, girl. I am grateful for everythin' people do for Aunt Clara. I will not fault Mr. Tabor for his rules and neither should you."

Katie knew that was the end of the discussion. Aunt Clara never had anything bad to say about anyone. Katie wished she could have her patience and love.

© Colorado Historical Society

*This girl is Anna or Eugenia Kennicott, but Katie O'Brien might very well have looked much the same when she worked for Aunt Clara Brown.*

Colorado Historical Society, 10028877

## Chapter 16
# CHIEF LITTLE RAVEN VISITS

Katie and Mrs. Neal continued their chores and saw to the needs of Aunt Clara. There was a knock on the door one day, and ever-curious Katie went to answer it. There stood the strangest sight she had ever seen. Katie was used to Aunt Clara's friends, both white and black; but this old gentleman was a dark-skinned Indian with long black hair. He wore an Army coat with Indian leggings and a white Indian breechcloth. He carried a black-and-white cane. He stood straight, but Katie thought he must be well past seventy years of age.

"Mrs. Brown, I want to see," he spoke.

Katie, remembering her manners asked, "Who should I tell her is callin'?"

"Tell White-Haired Lady it is Chief Little Raven come to call."

"Please step inside the door, and I will tell Aunt Clara you are here."

Katie walked quickly to the parlor. "Aunt Clara, Aunt Clara, there's an Indian to see you."

"Oh, that must be old Little Raven. He's always out and about these days, visitin' some of us old folks who saw Denver grow up. Bring him in."

The oddly dressed Indian entered the parlor and looked around for a place to sit. He finally sat down upon the carpet near Aunt Clara's rocking chair. Katie thought he had good sense to avoid sitting on that stiff horsehair sofa.

"Katie, why don't you stay with us and talk to my friend, Little Raven?"

*Little Raven, the Arapaho Indian, who visited Aunt Clara Brown.*
Denver Public Library, Western History Department, X-32369

Katie needed no coaxing to join the conversation. She, too, sat on the floor near Little Raven. He smiled as they both sat cross-legged near Aunt Clara.

Little Raven was the first to speak. "How are you, Mrs. Brown? Hear you haven't been feeling well."

"Oh, I can't complain. I've got Katie and Mrs. Neal to help me. I've got friends like you droppin' by. I can see the world go by my window. I'm sittin' pretty in my rockin' chair. I just miss gettin' out to help others."

"The word at my teepee is that you are special lady. We old-timers must take care of each other. I can remember early days when the Arapaho warriors hunted and traded near the rivers. I tried to be friends with white men who wanted gold, but I think people like you are the heart of Denver."

"Chief Little Raven, you honor me with your words and with your visit. You know my father was a full-blooded Cherokee Indian, so I have a real special feelin' for you and your people," stated Aunt Clara.

"That's all I have to say," ended Little Raven as he rose from the floor, bowed to Aunt Clara, and made his way to the door.

It was over so quickly that Katie had had no time to ask him about his adventures. He was a man of few words.

## Chapter 17
# A NEW CONTRAPTION

One day Katie was shaking some rugs on Aunt Clara's front porch when she noticed the next-door neighbor lady getting onto a contraption that could only be called 'strange.'

"Mrs. Adams, Mrs. Adams," Katie said.

"Hello, Katie, how's Mrs. Brown?"

"She's fine, but I'd like to know what that thing is you've got," Katie asked.

"Oh, this is my fitness machine. She walked over with the two-wheeled mechanism, set it against the porch railing, and sat down on the step. "Come join me, and I'll tell you all about it."

Katie was glad to take a break from her chores. She sat down next to Mrs. Adams, leaned her elbows on her lap, and put her chin in her hands to listen to Mrs. Adams' story.

"It's hard to believe, Katie, but not too long ago I was a consumptive. That means I had breathing problems. I heard Denver was the best place to come if I wanted to survive, because the climate is so dry here. I could breathe a lot easier. I went to Doctor McClelland's clinic. He was from Ohio, just like me. Anyway, I had to stay in bed a long time, usually out in the fresh air and sunshine. It took a while, but with Dr. McClelland's kind care, I was cured. The doctor advised me to get a lot of exercise for my lungs, so I took up cycling. I've been cycling all around Denver for about a year. I'm even thinking of entering a century."

"What's that?" asked Katie.

"It's a tough bicycle ride of one hundred miles in one day," announced Mrs. Adams proudly.

"One hundred miles, one day! You must be a strong lady!" Katie said.

"I don't know about that. I do know I love to cycle. It makes me feel free, and I know it's good for my health. I'm even thinking of buying a divided skirt instead of these old ankle-length skirts that get caught in the bicycle chain and cause me to tumble. I know it will be the talk of the neighborhood, because proper ladies aren't supposed to show their ankles, but I don't care. I want to be safe and comfortable.

"Katie, you might even want to try out this bicycle. How'd you like that?"

"Oh, could I?" exclaimed Katie.

"Here, let me help you up. Why don't you stand on the lowest porch step and swing yourself over the seat, grab the handlebars, and start pedaling? I'll even help you get started by holding onto the seat. It's not always so easy learning to balance, but once you get the idea, there's no stopping you."

Katie did as she was told. She wobbled down the street with Mrs. Adams holding onto the seat. In the second block, Mrs. Adams let go, and Katie found that she could balance without any help.

She waved back at Mrs. Adams, swerved a bit, and lost control. Luckily she landed in a grassy yard. Mrs. Adams came running, "Are you all right, Katie?"

"I sure am, Mrs. Adams! I see what you mean about feelin' free. It's as if I had wings. I love it!"

"You're welcome to ride my bicycle any time you wish, Katie, as long as you have permission from Mrs. Neal and Mrs. Brown."

"Thanks a lot. I've been saving my earnings for somethin' special. Now I know what that somethin' special is going to be — a bicycle. Why I might even save some money for a divided skirt just like yours!"

## Chapter 18
# AUNT CLARA'S GRANDDAUGHTER ARRIVES

"Cindy's comin'! Cindy's comin'!" Aunt Clara yelled from the parlor. Both Mrs. Neal and Katie ran into the room, thinking she was having another sick spell.

"This note says Cindy is travelin' all the way from Council Bluffs to spend time with her old grandmother. I can't believe it! It's too much!"

"Now Mrs. Brown, take it easy," warned Mrs. Neal. "You don't want to have another spell."

"Oh, I know, but I can hardly wait for her to come. Eliza Jane says her daughter will be comin' in a month. We must fix up the house — clean, wash, and dust everythin', so we're ready when she arrives."

"Now you just rest. Katie and I will see to the chores," Mrs. Neal said. "We will make a plan to have this house shining and clean by the time Cindy arrives."

And so it was. Mrs. Neal and Katie worked at shaking the rugs, sweeping the floors, dusting the furniture, washing the dishes and silverware, shopping for the best foods. Katie was exhausted by the end of the days leading up to Cindy's visit. There wasn't even time to ride Mrs. Adams' bicycle as she'd hoped. She still thought about buying one for herself, but that would have to wait until later.

Finally the big day arrived, and Aunt Clara would not hear of staying home.

"Katie and I will meet her at Union Depot. You stay home and rest," urged Mrs. Neal.

"No, no, I'll not hear of it. I must be the first to greet my Cindy," Aunt Clara insisted.

Mrs. Neal and Katie went with Aunt Clara, who stubbornly hobbled up to the platform at Union Station. The train was due to arrive at 10:45. They peered into the distance looking for the smoking engine and the sound of its whistle.

After what seemed a long time, the train pulled into the station from the east. The conductor quickly stepped out with his stepstool to help the passengers alight. There were gentlemen in business suits, women with children, but no Cindy.

"No, wait. There she is!" shouted Aunt Clara.

Sure enough, the last passenger to step down was a dark-skinned girl dressed in a long skirt with an over-jacket that buttoned snugly at the waist. She had black gloves and shoes. Her hair was pulled back with a ribbon. Katie thought she was the prettiest girl she had ever seen in all her fine clothes.

"Cindy, Cindy, we're over here!" Aunt Clara yelled.

Cindy turned with a smile and waved at the three people standing down the track. It was her grandmother and two others, one on each side, holding an arm. Cindy ran the length of the platform and hugged her grandmother.

"Oh, Grandma, it's so good to see you. We'll finally have a chance to get to know each other," she exclaimed.

And that's how it was. Cindy and Aunt Clara talked and talked all day long until the old woman fell asleep.

Katie was excited to have a guest that loved Aunt Clara as much as she did, but part of her was jealous. No longer were there times when Katie, all by herself, could sit at Aunt Clara's knee to hear all about her adventures.

It seemed that Cindy was going to stay a long time. It was Cindy who walked down to Baur's for the special sodas Aunt Clara loved. It was Cindy who tucked the blanket around Aunt Clara's knees. It was Cindy who sat in the parlor, listening to the stories Aunt Clara loved to tell.

Katie did get more free time for reading and riding Mrs. Adams' bicycle. One time Mrs. Adams had even borrowed a bicycle from a friend, so that the two of them could go cycling down near Cherry Creek. It had been a long trip, but they had packed a picnic lunch and eaten it along the creek bank. They had ridden further northwest to where Cherry Creek and the South Platte River met.

"This is where gold was first discovered. Denver City started right here with tents and shacks all around."

"It must have been hard to paddle a canoe or a boat around here with all the swirling water," Katie thought.

When Katie returned home, it was a pleasant memory to tell Mrs. Neal, Aunt Clara, and Cindy around the kitchen table.

"It was great to have the wind blowin' in my hair. Mrs. Adams even showed me where the first gold was discovered; we ate a picnic lunch that she'd packed and put on the back of her bicycle," Katie related to the interested women.

"I know I'm goin' to buy myself a new bicycle as soon as I can."

"It sounds as if you've found that somethin' special you've been lookin' for, honey," said Aunt Clara.

One day, just when Katie thought Cindy would never leave, she announced that she would have to head back to Council Bluffs.

"It has been months already. I don't want to be a nuisance, and Mama needs me back in Council Bluffs to help take care of all my brothers and sisters."

Katie began to feel a little bit guilty because she had missed Aunt Clara's attention, but now that Cindy had said she was leaving, Katie knew she would miss her. Cindy had been a big help. Katie knew Mrs. Neal was glad for the extra pair of hands.

"I rightly wish you could find it in your heart to stay, Cindy," Aunt Clara replied.

"Oh, Grandmother, I know how hard it is to part. I know Mother would like to make the trip as soon as she's able, but my eight brothers and sisters keep her busy." Aunt Clara seemed sad, but put on a smile and touched Cindy's arm.

"I know it's come to this. I've enjoyed your visit so much. You give my love to your mother. I can't believe I actually have family now. It's a blessin', for sure. You're welcome anytime. Just don't make it too long between visits," sighed Aunt Clara.

# Chapter 19
# AN INVITATION TO A
# SPECIAL PARTY

K atie answered the knock at the door. Standing on the porch was a dignified lady in black with a high lace collar and a bustle in the back. Once again Katie put her hand over her mouth. She didn't want to laugh right out loud. The bustle was a silly frill for women. It was a piece of fabric that covered an underskirt that women would wear to make their dresses stand out in the back. Usually there was also a bow or some such decoration to call attention to the thing. Katie thought the bustle made women look strange, as if there were more of them in the back than in the front.

The lady did have a serious look on her face. Katie knew she was on important business.

"Young lady, I'm here to see Mrs. Brown. My name is Mrs. Jacobs. Would you please announce me?"

Katie stammered, "Just a minute, please. Won't you step inside the door? Mrs. Brown has been feelin' poorly lately, but I know she'll be glad for company."

Katie entered the parlor and spoke gently into Aunt Clara's ear about a Mrs. Jacobs at the door.

"Why surely, show the fine lady into my parlor."

Katie led Mrs. Jacobs into the room, indicated the horsehair chair and left the room. Katie's curiosity got the better of her. She couldn't resist what such a fine lady would want with Aunt Clara. She peeked around the corner and neither woman noticed her; so Katie decided to stay hidden behind the curtain.

"Mrs. Brown, I am here to invite you to a special party in your honor. We of the Society of Colorado Pioneers would like to have a celebration of your life. You have helped so many people here, in Central City, and Kentucky. You brought ex-slaves here to settle in this pioneer town. You have helped start the first Sunday school. We are grateful and want to show our appreciation. Will you join us on March 6 at City Hall?"

Katie realized Aunt Clara was crying. The tears ran down her cheeks and for once she had nothing to say. Katie began to worry that maybe she would have an attack or fall out of her chair. Mr. Byer's wish had come true. The people of Denver were going to show their appreciation for all that Aunt Clara had done.

Then Aunt Clara recovered and spoke softly. "I'd be most honored to attend your party, Mrs. Jacobs," was all she could say. Mrs. Jacobs smiled, got up, and touched Aunt Clara on the arm.

"Thank you, Mrs. Brown. We'll see you soon."

"Maybe the fine lady wasn't so bad after all," thought Katie. Mrs. Jacobs had seemed so proper, but her heart was in her words to Aunt Clara. Katie couldn't be too upset about her silly bustle and fine airs, after all.

She stood at the door to see Mrs. Jacobs out. Mrs. Jacobs didn't even ask how Katie knew she was leaving. It didn't seem to occur to her that Katie might have heard every word that was said.

Katie walked back into the parlor and saw Aunt Clara glancing out the window, with the blanket over her knees. She noticed the old lady's ankles had swollen even more in the past few days. Katie thought it must be painful. The doctor had said there was nothing he could do, except to give her medicine for the pain. Aunt Clara never complained once.

"Aunt Clara, what a fine honor for you!" burst out Katie.

"Why I do believe little ears were listenin' to our conversation."

Katie blushed, but she knew Aunt Clara was only teasing.

# Chapter 20
# DENVER REMEMBERS AUNT CLARA

The big day arrived. Aunt Clara wore her best calico dress with a crisp white apron tied at the waist and a turban atop her head. Mrs. Neal was afraid the old woman would tire, but Aunt Clara was so excited, Mrs. Neal didn't want to say anything. Katie and Mrs. Neal had decided to go with Aunt Clara to help her with walking. They each took one arm and helped her into a waiting carriage.

When they arrived at City Hall, there was a host of people waiting to greet her. Mrs. Jacobs, the chairwoman for the event, had decided it would be best if Aunt Clara was seated in the lecture hall. People could give her their kind thoughts and regards while the guest of honor was seated in a comfortable chair.

Sure enough, the crowds of well-wishers came by. Katie and Mrs. Neal sat nearby, basking in the kind words that were offered Aunt Clara.

"Mrs. Brown, I do rightly remember when you brought me and my kinfolk all the way from old Kentucky. I'm makin' a livin' here as a laundress and a seamstress. My daughter even has a job as a maid for a rich family. I thank you, kind lady."

Aunt Clara beamed with pleasure. "I was only doin' what I thought was right. I'm glad to hear you're prosperin'."

Finally, it was time for dinner. Katie and Mrs. Neal each took an arm and sat Aunt Clara at a banquet table at the front of the room. After dinner the fun began, because the master of ceremonies began to tell about Aunt Clara's accomplishments.

> "We have come here this evening to pay honor to Mrs. Aunt Clara Brown. This fine lady was born into slavery in Spotsylvania, Virginia, near Fredericksburg. All of us remember Fredericksburg as the site of that terrible Civil War battle.

> "At the age of nine, she and her mother were taken to Kentucky. She married at eighteen and had four children. When she was thirty-five, she was separated from her dear children and husband. She was freed by her third owner in 1859 and came West as a laundress with a wagon train.

"It was this fine lady's desire to bring other slaves to freedom. She worked as a laundress in Central City, charging fifty cents a garment to wash miners' dirty clothes. She saved her money to help others, never thinking of herself.

"She even went back to Kentucky to get other ex-slaves and bring them to Colorado, all the while looking for her four children. Sadly, she has found only one daughter in Council Bluffs, Iowa. Her name is Eliza Jane Brewer. Mrs. Brewer is the sole support for nine children because her husband died during the War. Eliza Jane could not be with us tonight.

"It is with great honor that we present Aunt Clara Brown with this envelope of money from thankful Colorado citizens who wish to honor her."

He then handed Aunt Clara an envelope stuffed with money. She was so surprised that all she could do was nod and smile. It was hard for her to stand, but she did with Katie's and Mrs. Neal's help.

"I want to thank all of my friends who came tonight. I thank you for your kind wishes. The money will go toward makin' my life a bit more comfortable for the remainin' time I have left."

With that simple thank-you, she sat down. The hall erupted into wild applause. Katie clapped so loudly her hands stung. She was so proud that she blushed to think she knew such a fine lady.

# Chapter 21
## AUNT CLARA TELLS THE STORY ABOUT MEETING HER DAUGHTER

Aunt Clara was tired and went right to bed after the big celebration. In fact, she slept most of the next day, too. Katie knew she had enjoyed the evening because it was all she could talk about on her way home.

When Aunt Clara had recovered and was sitting in her usual place by the parlor window, Katie approached her. "Aunt Clara, I'm wonderin' about one thing in that wonderful speech that was given in your honor the other night."

"What is it, child?"

"I've felt so lonely without a mother and father. Then my brother Joe was adopted by a family and I didn't go to the same home.

"You and I are a lot alike. I lost my brother, but you lost your whole family. I hope some day I'll be lucky enough to find Joe again, just like you found Eliza Jane and Cindy.

"Tell me about all those years of lookin' for your children, when you found your daughter. What was it like to find her?"

"Oh, child, it was the most wonderful feelin' in the whole world. I couldn't believe a friend of mine in Council Bluffs had actually met my dear Eliza Jane. It really is a special story. Do you have time from your chores to listen to an old lady's story?"

Katie nodded her head.

"I really was gettin' low in money when my friend told me to come to Council Bluffs, but people were so kind to this white-haired woman. I owe special thanks to the Union Pacific Railroad and the good folks at the Central Presbyterian Church. Reverend Clelland and his congregation in Council Bluffs helped me, too. I was able to buy new clothes and ride the railroad to see my long-lost Eliza Jane and her family. I was so pleased with everyone's help and kindness that I put a thank-you in the newspaper. It was the only way I could properly thank everyone who'd helped me. I don't read and write much, so a reporter wrote my letter for me."

Aunt Clara was in tears, and Katie was afraid all of these memories were too much for her. But she continued with a smile on her wrinkled face:

"The funniest thing was how Eliza Jane and I finally did meet. Everyone has a good laugh when I tell them about it. It seems there was a big rain right before I came, so the streets were muddy. I saw Eliza Jane in the distance. She was runnin' late. We both saw each other at the same time and started runnin' toward each other. Wouldn't you know that old mud reached up and almost sucked us up? It was funny to see both of us fall in that old mud, but we didn't care. We had finally found each other. We hugged and hugged."

Katie's mouth had dropped open with this new story from Aunt Clara. Was there no end to this woman's tales? Katie quickly put her arms around the old woman to hug her.

"You are the best lady I know, Aunt Clara!"

"Oh, honey, I don't think I've done more than most would have done in my shoes."

"Oh, yes you have. You have spent most of your money on others. You are loved by all who know you. Look at the party Denver gave you. You have lived such an excitin' life."

"Oh, shucks, you make an old lady happy, Katie."

## Chapter 22
# KATIE AND AUNT CLARA

Katie was soon back to her chores — helping Mrs. Neal with the cooking, cleaning, and washing. It was hard work. Katie didn't mind because once she was finished, she could talk to Aunt Clara. Sometimes the old lady was taking a nap by the window. Sometimes Katie would find her daydreaming with the patchwork blanket over her knees. Sometimes Katie would just sit by Aunt Clara and lean her head in her lap. She was the closest Katie had ever come to having a grandmother. In her heart Katie knew there wasn't much time for the dear lady. She had been born into slavery. She had gained her freedom. She had helped other ex-slaves to make a home in Colorado. She had worked hard as a washerwoman. She had saved money to help others. She had found one of her children. She had brought Mrs. Neal and Katie to Denver to care for her. She had friends who loved her.

Katie would daydream about her future as Aunt Clara slept peacefully in the chair. Because Aunt Clara had found part of her family, Katie knew in her heart she would find Joe once again. She would travel on a train, just like Aunt Clara had done. She and Joe would be brother and sister once again. Katie was sure. And she knew, by golly, that she'd save her money and get that bicycle just like Mrs. Adams' contraption. She had dreams of riding in a century, taking the grand-prize trophy, and being in one of the cycling magazines Mrs. Adams had shown her.

But most of all, Katie knew Aunt Clara's good deeds would be remembered. She was an amazing lady and had helped Katie feel at home in Denver. She had offered her kindness and her home to a sad little orphan. She was a grand lady!

*(Author's note: Aunt Clara died on October 23, 1885. There was a large funeral for her at the Central Presbyterian Church. The mayor of Denver, John L. Routt, and Colorado's governor, James B. Grant, attended the service which was conducted by The Colorado Pioneer Association. She had been their first African-American member. She was buried in Riverside Cemetery. There is a stained-glass window in her honor in the State Capitol building.)*

# ACTIVITY PAGE

1. Find ten words in the story that you do not know. Look up their definitions and put the words in alphabetical order.

2. Choose one of the real-life characters in the story and find out more about him or her. Suggestions: General William Larimer, William Byers, Barney Ford, Baby Doe Tabor.

3. Draw a map of early Denver. Place Cherry Creek and the South Platte River on the map. What were the names of some of the early streets in Denver? What streets are the same in Denver today?

4. Trace the trip that Katie O'Brien traveled from New York City to Omaha, Nebraska to Council Bluffs, Iowa to Denver, Colorado. Can you figure out how many miles she traveled?

5. Write a sequel (a continuation) of the story of Katie O'Brien.

6. Take a tour of Lower Downtown where the old city began. Can you find a marker for Barney Ford's building, for the Union Station?

7. Write about a day in the life of Katie O'Brien. What would she do? What would she wear? Where would she go?

8. Pretend to write a story about Aunt Clara Brown as if you are Aunt Clara herself. Suggestions: What would be Aunt Clara's reactions to living during the Civil War? How would she feel about the great honor she received from the people of Denver? What would it have been like to live in a gold-rush town, such as Central City?

9. Find out more about the Orphan Train that brought Katie to Omaha, Nebraska. You might even want to read "The Orphan Train Series" by Joan Lowery Nixon.

10. The bicycle Katie rode was a fairly new idea. Look for pictures of other old cycles. What did they look like? Draw a picture of one.